D1095575

First Facts

SUPER SCARY STUFF

SUPER SCARY PLACES

BY MEGAN COOLEY PETERSON

CAPSTONE PRESS
a capstone imprint

First Facts are published by Capstone Press,
1710 Roe Crest Drive, North Mankato, Minnesota 56003
www.mycapstone.com

Library of Congress Cataloging-in-Publication Data
Names: Peterson, Megan Cooley, author.
Title: Super scary places / by Megan Cooley Peterson.
Description: North Mankato, Minnesota : First Facts are published by Capstone
 Press, [2017] | Series: First facts. Super scary stuff | Includes
 bibliographical references and index.
Identifiers: LCCN 2015041215 | ISBN 9781515702788 (library binding) | ISBN
 9781515702825 (ebook pdf)
Subjects: LCSH: Haunted places—Juvenile literature.
Classification: LCC BF1461 .P4375 2017 | DDC 133.1/2—dc23
LC record available at http://lccn.loc.gov/2015041215

Editorial Credits
Carrie Braulick Sheely, editor; Kyle Grenz, designer; Svetlana Zhurkin, media researcher;
 Katy LaVigne, production specialist

Photo Credits
Dreamstime: Russiangal, 15; Getty Images: WireImage/Barry King, 17; Newscom: Photoshot/
NHPA/Mark O'Shea, 9; Shutterstock: Bertl123, 21, CPbackpacker, 18, Gail Johnson, cover, 13,
ID1974, 5, javarman, 11, observe.co, 1, soft_light, 19; SuperStock: Marsden Archive, 7

Design Elements by Shutterstock

Printed and bound in China.
007702

TABLE OF CONTENTS

ENTER IF YOU DARE!

Haunted houses. Caves crawling with bugs. Underground tunnels filled with human bones. Some places make you shake with fear. Are you feeling brave? Come along on a tour of some of the world's scariest places.

Places may be haunted by more than *spirits* of people. Animal *ghosts* and even ghost ships have been reported.

haunted—having mysterious events happen often, possibly because of visits from ghosts

spirit—the soul or invisible part of a person that is believed to control thoughts and feelings; some people believe the spirit leaves the body after death

ghost—a spirit of a dead person believed to haunt places

ENGLAND'S MOST HAUNTED HOUSE

Borley Rectory was once called England's most haunted house. People reported objects moving on their own. A headless ghost was seen walking through the bushes. Borley's most famous ghost was a *nun*. People often saw her roaming the grounds. The house burned down in 1939.

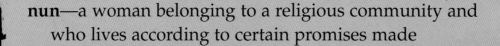

nun—a woman belonging to a religious community and who lives according to certain promises made

Harry Price

Harry Price was a famous early ghost hunter. In the 1930s he studied the hauntings at Borley. His books described the ghostly events reported in the house. Price was later accused of faking some of his findings. No one knows if his Borley reports are true.

In 1944 a reporter and photographer visited the Borley Rectory ruins. They claimed a brick floated more than 4 feet (1.2 meters) above the remains.

A DEADLY ISLAND

Imagine stepping onto Snake Island in Brazil. Thousands of slithering golden lancehead vipers snap at your feet. Their *venom* can melt human flesh.

These lanceheads are found only on Snake Island. Luckily, the Brazilian government has banned travel to the island.

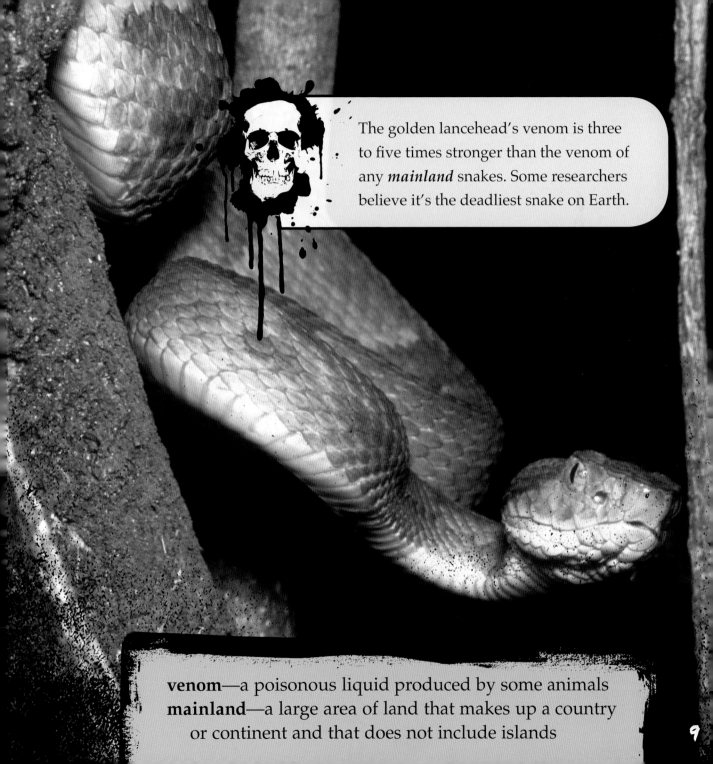

The golden lancehead's venom is three to five times stronger than the venom of any *mainland* snakes. Some researchers believe it's the deadliest snake on Earth.

venom—a poisonous liquid produced by some animals
mainland—a large area of land that makes up a country or continent and that does not include islands

THE PARIS CATACOMBS

Beneath the streets of Paris, France, lies a maze of bones called the catacombs. The remains of about 6 million people line the twisting walls.

This giant underground cemetery began as a rock *quarry*. In the late 1700s, Paris graveyards grew too full. The dead were moved into the quarry. Today visitors can tour the tunnels—if they dare.

quarry—a place where stone or other minerals are dug from the ground

The Cemetery of the Innocents was the first graveyard moved into the Paris Catacombs. It took two years to move all the bones.

GETTING CHILLS AT CHILLINGHAM

Long ago prisoners were punished and killed at Chillingham Castle. Ghosts have reportedly haunted this English castle ever since. People report objects moving on their own. The ghost of a boy dressed in blue wakes visitors with his screams. A ghostly woman appears in the pantry.

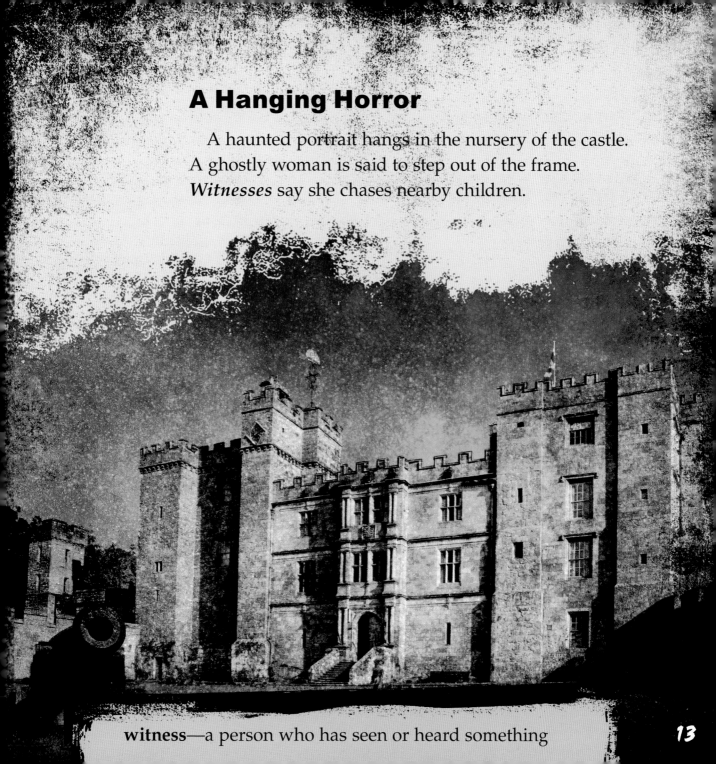

A Hanging Horror

A haunted portrait hangs in the nursery of the castle. A ghostly woman is said to step out of the frame. *Witnesses* say she chases nearby children.

witness—a person who has seen or heard something

THE HOUSE BUILT FOR GHOSTS

Some people say Winchester House in San Jose, California, was built for ghosts. The Winchester family made rifles. When Sarah Winchester's husband died in 1881, she said she contacted his ghost. His ghost told her spirits of people killed by Winchester rifles had *cursed* the family. To make these ghosts happy, Sarah had to build them a house.

Spooky Séance

A *medium* held a *séance* at Winchester House after Sarah Winchester died. Witnesses claimed the medium's hair suddenly turned gray and that wrinkles lined her face. After the séance her face appeared normal again.

curse—to cast an evil spell meant to harm someone
medium—a person who claims to make contact with ghosts
séance—a meeting at which people try to make contact with the dead

Over the next 38 years, Sarah built a 160-room house. Its mazelike layout may have been meant to confuse the ghosts. Doors opened into solid walls. Staircases led to nowhere.

Visitors have reported many mysterious events. They have felt cold spots and seen blazing balls of light. Some claimed to have seen the ghost of Sarah Winchester.

Winchester House has 10,000 windows, 47 fireplaces, and 13 bathrooms.

CREEPY CRAWLIES

Don't wander into Gomantong Cave without a flashlight. This cave in Malaysia houses millions of bats. Billions of cockroaches feed on piles of bat poop reaching nearly 100 feet (30 meters) tall. Poisonous centipedes scurry along cave walls, gobbling up the cockroaches. That's one creepy *food chain*.

Gomantong Cave smells terrible. As the bat poop breaks down, strong-smelling ammonia gas is released.

food chain—a series of animals in which each one in the series eats the one before it

A GHASTLY GRAVEYARD

Think twice before visiting Greyfriars Kirkyard Cemetery in Scotland. Beginning in the 1560s, part of this cemetery was a prison. Many prisoners died there. Today visitors report being bitten and scratched by unseen forces. Some believe the ghost of lawyer George Mackenzie haunts the graveyard. He sent many people to the prison.

Creepy places exist around the world. Each one has its own horrors to reveal. Would you dare to visit any yourself?

In 1999 a man broke into George Mackenzie's *mausoleum*. Some people believe the man released Mackenzie's ghost.

mausoleum—a large building that holds tombs

GLOSSARY

curse (KURS)—to cast an evil spell meant to harm someone

food chain (FOOD CHAYN)—a series of organisms in which each one in the series eats the one before it

ghost (GOHST)—a spirit of a dead person believed to haunt places

haunted (HAWN-ted)—having mysterious events happen often, possibly because of visits from ghosts

mainland (MAYN-land)—a large area of land that makes up a country or continent and that does not include islands

mausoleum (maw-suh-LEE-uhm)—a large building that holds tombs

medium (MEE-dee-uhm)—a person who claims to make contact with ghosts

nun (NUN)—a woman belonging to a religious community and who lives according to certain promises made

quarry (KWOR-ee)—a place where stone or other minerals are dug from the ground

séance (SAY-ahnss)—a meeting at which people try to make contact with the dead

spirit (SPIHR-it)—the soul or invisible part of a person that is believed to control thoughts and feelings; some people believe the spirit leaves the body after death

venom (VEN-uhm)—a poisonous liquid produced by some animals

witness (WIT-nes)—a person who has seen or heard something

READ MORE

Polydoros, Lori. *Top 10 Haunted Places.* Top 10 Unexplained. North Mankato, Minn.: Capstone Press, 2012.

Raij, Emily. *The Most Haunted Places in the World.* Spooked! North Mankato, Minn.: Capstone Press, 2016.

Taylor, Troy. *Creepy Libraries.* Scary Places. New York: Bearport Publishing, 2016.

INTERNET SITES

FactHound offers a safe, fun way to find Internet sites related to this book. All of the sites on FactHound have been researched by our staff.

Here's all you do:

Visit *www.facthound.com*

Type in this code: 9781515702788

Super-cool stuff!

Check out projects, games and lots more at
www.capstonekids.com

INDEX